PERRAULT'S FAIRY TALES

PERRAULT'S FAIRY TALES

Translated from the French
by Sasha Moorsom

Illustrated by Landa Crommelynck

Doubleday & Company, Inc., Garden City, New York

LIBRARY OF CONGRESS CATALOG CARD NUMBER: 76-131306
TRANSLATION COPYRIGHT © 1972
BY SASHA YOUNG
ILLUSTRATIONS COPYRIGHT © 1972
BY LANDA CROMMELYNCK
PRINTED IN THE UNITED STATES OF AMERICA
FIRST EDITION

CONTENTS

STORIES OF OLDEN TIMES

Little Red Ridinghood

Once upon a time there was a little village girl, the prettiest you could hope to see. Her mother loved her dearly and her grandmother even more. The kind old lady had a little red ridinghood made for her and it suited her so well that everyone called her Little Red Ridinghood.

One day when her mother had baked some cakes she said to her:

"Go and see how your grandmother is because I heard she was ill. Take her a cake and this little pot of butter."

Little Red Ridinghood set off at once to go and see her grandmother who lived in another village. On her way through the wood she met Mr. Wolf. He would have liked to eat her up but he did not dare because there were some woodcutters nearby in the forest. He asked her where she was going. The poor child did not know that it is dangerous to stop and talk to a wolf and she said:

"I'm going to see my grandmother to take her a cake and a little pot of butter from my mother."

"Does she live far away?" asked the wolf.

"Oh yes," said Little Red Ridinghood, "it's past the mill that you can see over there. Hers is the first house in the village."

"Good," said the wolf, "I'd like to go and see her too. I'll take this path and you take that one and we'll see who gets there first."

The wolf ran off as fast as he could along the shortest path and the little girl took the longest path. She enjoyed herself, gathering nuts, chasing butterflies and picking bunches of wild flowers as she went.

The wolf did not take long to get to the grandmother's house. He banged on the door: knock, knock.

"Who's there?"

"It's your granddaughter, Little Red Ridinghood," said the wolf, imitating her voice. "I've brought you a cake and a little pot of butter from my mother."

The poor grandmother, who was in bed because she did not feel very well, called out:

"Lift the latch and the door will open."

The wolf lifted the latch and the door opened. He sprang at the old lady and gobbled her up at once because he had had nothing to eat for three days. Then he shut the door and got into the grandmother's bed to wait for Little Red Ridinghood. A little while later she arrived and banged on the door: knock, knock.

"Who's there?"

When Little Red Ridinghood heard the wolf's gruff voice she was afraid. Then, thinking her grandmother must have a cold, she answered:

"It's your granddaughter, Little Red Ridinghood. I've brought you a cake and a little pot of butter from my mother."

Then the wolf softened his voice a little and called out:

"Lift the latch and the door will open."

Little Red Ridinghood lifted the latch and the door opened.

When the wolf saw her coming in, he hid under the bedclothes and said:

"Put the cake and the little pot of butter on the bread bin and come and lie down beside me."

Little Red Ridinghood took off her things and got into bed. She was so surprised to see what her grandmother looked like undressed that she said to her:

"Grandmother, what big arms you have!"

"All the better to hug you with, my dear."

"Grandmother, what big legs you have!"

"All the better to run with, my child."

"Grandmother, what big ears you have!"

"All the better to hear with, my child."

"Grandmother, what big eyes you have!"

"All the better to see with, my child."

"Grandmother, what big teeth you have!"

"All the better to gobble you up."

With these words the wicked wolf sprang at Little Red Ridinghood and ate her up.

MORAL

This story shows that little girls
So pretty, kind and neat
Should never stop and talk to any
Stranger that they meet.
For if they do the wolf will pounce
And eat these morsels up at once.

I say the wolf, but don't forget
All wolves are not the same,
For there are some that don't seem fierce,
Pretending to be tame.
But oh, beware, for you will find
These wolves are the most dangerous kind.

Bluebeard

ONCE UPON A TIME there was a man who owned many fine houses both in the town and the country. He had dishes of gold and silver, richly embroidered furnishings and golden carriages. But by ill luck this man had a blue beard. It made him look so ugly and frightening that both women and girls ran away at the sight of him.

One of his neighbors was a well-born lady who had two most beautiful daughters. He asked her to give him one of them in marriage, leaving her to choose which one it should be. Neither of them wanted anything to do with him, and they argued back and forth about it. They could not bring themselves to accept a man with a blue beard. What put them off even more was the fact that he had already been married several times. But no one knew what had become of his other wives.

In order to get to know them, Bluebeard invited the girls and their mother and three or four of their best friends and some young men from the district to come and spend a week in one of his country houses. They spent the time in going for walks, in hunting and fishing, dancing and feasting. They never slept but all night long they joked and played tricks on each other. In fact it all went so well that the younger daughter began to think that their host's beard was not so blue after all and he was really rather a likeable fellow. As soon as they got back to town the marriage was arranged.

After a month Bluebeard said to his wife that he had to go on a journey for six weeks or more on some important business. He told her to enjoy herself while he was away, to invite her friends and take them to the country if she wanted to and give them a good time.

"Here," he said, "are the keys of the two big storerooms; these are for the gold

and silver plate that is not used for every day; these are for my strongboxes where I keep my gold and silver; these are for the jewel cases full of precious stones; and this is the master key of all the rooms. As for this little key, it is the key to the little room at the end of the long gallery on the ground floor. Unlock everything, go wherever you like except into this little room. I forbid you to enter it. I forbid you absolutely. If by any chance you should happen to open it there would be no bounds to my rage."

She promised to do exactly as he had said. Then he kissed her, got into his carriage and went off on his journey.

Her neighbors and friends did not wait to be invited to visit the young bride. They were eager to see all the riches in her house. They had not dared to come

and see her when her husband was there because they were afraid of his blue beard. Now they rushed into all the rooms, each one more magnificent than the last. They went up into the storerooms and marveled at all the beautiful tapestries, the beds, the sofas, the cupboards and the tables. The mirrors were the most magnificent they had ever seen, long enough to reflect them from head to foot with frames of cut glass or gold and silver. They could not help being envious of their friend's good fortune. But all this time she hardly noticed these riches because she was so impatient to go and open the little room on the ground floor.

She was so eaten up with curiosity that, without thinking how rude it was to leave her guests, she went down a little secret staircase. She went so fast that she nearly tripped and broke her neck two or three times. When she got to the door of the little room she stopped for a moment, remembering her husband's orders. She wondered whether something bad might happen to her if she disobeyed. But the temptation was too great to resist. So she took the little key and with trembling fingers unlocked the door of the little room.

At first she could see nothing because the shutters were closed. But after a little while she began to see that the floor was covered with clots of blood, and in the blood were reflected the bodies of several dead women hanging on the walls. These were Bluebeard's other wives. He had married them and then cut their throats one after another. She thought she would die of fright. They key of the little room, that she had just taken out of the lock, fell from her hand. When she had recovered herself a little she picked up the key, locked the door again and went up to her room to try to get over it. But she was so upset she could not forget it.

Noticing that the key of the little room was stained with blood, she wiped it two or three times. But the blood would not go away. She washed it and even scrubbed it with sand and grit. The blood was still there. It was a magic key. There was no way of getting it quite clean. When the blood was washed off one side, it came back on the other.

Bluebeard came back from his journey that very same evening, saying that on the way he had received letters telling him that his business had already been arranged satisfactorily. His wife did the best she could to make it seem as if she was delighted by his quick return.

The next day he asked her for the keys and she gave them back to him. But her hand was shaking so much that he guessed at once what had happened.

"How is it," he said, "that the key to the little room is not here?"

"I must have left it upstairs on my table," she said.

"Don't forget to give it to me soon," said Bluebeard.

After putting him off several times, she finally had to bring him the key. Bluebeard looked at it carefully, then said to his wife:

"Why is there blood on this key?"

16

"I have no idea," replied the poor woman going paler than death.

"*You* have no idea," said Bluebeard, "but I have. You tried to go into the little room. Well, madam, in you will go. You will take your place next to the other ladies you saw there."

She threw herself at her husband's feet, weeping and begging his forgiveness, showing how sorry she was to have disobeyed him. She was so sad and beautiful that she would have melted a stone. But Bluebeard's heart was harder than a stone.

"You must die, madam," he said, "and at once!"

"Since I must die," she replied, looking at him with her eyes full of tears, "give me a little time to say my prayers."

"I will give you five minutes," said Bluebeard, "but not a moment longer."

As soon as she was alone she called her sister and said to her:

"Sister Anne"—for that was her name—"go up to the top of the tower, I beg you, to see if my brothers are coming. They promised to come and see me today. If you see them, beckon to them to hurry."

Sister Anne went up to the top of the tower, and every few minutes the poor young bride called out to her:

"Anne, sister Anne, do you see anyone coming?"

And sister Anne replied:

"Only the sun shining down and the green grass growing."

Meanwhile Bluebeard, with his big sword in his hand, shouted out to his wife:

"Come down at once or I shall come up!"

"Just a moment longer," answered his wife. Then she called softly:

"Anne, sister Anne, do you see anyone coming?"

And sister Anne replied:

"Only the sun shining down and the green grass growing."

"Come down at once," shouted Bluebeard, "or I shall come up."

"I'm coming," said his wife, and then she called out:

"Anne, sister Anne, do you see anyone coming?"

"I can see a big cloud of dust coming from over there," replied sister Anne.

"Is it my brothers?"

"Alas no, sister, it's only a flock of sheep."

"Will you come down?" shouted Bluebeard.

"Just a moment more," replied his wife and then she called:

"Anne, sister Anne, do you see anyone coming?"

"I see two horsemen coming from over there," she replied, "but they are still a long way off. . . . God be praised!" she cried out a moment later. "It's our brothers. I'll beckon as hard as I can to hurry them up."

Bluebeard began to shout so loudly that the whole house shook. The poor girl came downstairs and threw herself at his feet, wild with weeping.

"That will do you no good," said Bluebeard, "you must die." Seizing her by the hair and raising his sword in the air, he was just about to cut off her head. The poor girl looked at him with dying eyes and begged him to give her a moment more to collect herself.

"No, no," he said as he raised his arm. "Commend your soul to God." At that moment there was such a knocking at the gate that Bluebeard stopped short. The gate was opened and two horsemen with swords in their hands rushed straight at Bluebeard.

He recognized his wife's brothers, both of them brave soldiers, and tried to escape to save himself. But the two brothers were so close behind him that they caught him before he could reach the steps. They ran him through with their swords and left him dead. The poor bride was hardly more alive than he was. She had not even the strength to get up and kiss her brothers.

It turned out that Bluebeard had no heirs, so all his riches went to his wife. She used some of it to marry her sister Anne to a young man who had been in love with her for a long time. With another part she bought captain's commissions for her two brothers. With the rest she herself married a fine young man who made her forget the horrible time she had had with Bluebeard.

FIRST MORAL

The charms of curiosity are great
But cause us sorrow if we follow them
As many stories daily demonstrate.
The pleasure that it brings lasts but a moment
Then fades away as soon as it is known,
A brief delight that always costs too dear.

SECOND MORAL

If you know something of the world
You'll guess this story that I've told
Is one that happened long ago;
A little sense will tell you so.
For husbands aren't so fierce today,
They don't make rules you can't obey,
And even if they're sometimes cross
They don't insist on being boss.
However blue their beards may be
They're no more cruel than you or me.

The Fairies

Once upon a time there was a widow with two daughters. The oldest one was just like her mother in looks and character. They were both so stuck-up and bad tempered that no one could stand them. The youngest was gentle and good-natured like her father. Besides this she was one of the most beautiful girls you could hope to see. As people naturally like those who are like themselves, the mother doted on her oldest daughter. But she really hated the youngest. She made her eat in the kitchen and work like a slave.

One of the jobs this poor child had to do was to go twice a day to fetch water some miles from the house. She had to carry it back in a big jug. One day when she was at the fountain, a poor woman came up to her and begged her for a drink.

"Of course," said the lovely girl. She rinsed out her jug, filled it with fresh water from the fountain and offered it to her. She held it up to make it easier for her to drink.

When she had drunk, the good woman said to her:

"You are so beautiful and so kind that I want to make you a gift." (She was a fairy who had taken the shape of a poor village woman to test the girl's kindness.) "The gift that I give you," went on the fairy, "is that each time you speak, a flower or a precious stone will fall from your mouth."

When the beautiful girl arrived home, her mother began to scold her for being so long at the fountain.

"I am so sorry, Mother, for being so long," said the poor girl. As she spoke, two roses, two pearls and two large diamonds fell out of her mouth.

"What's this?" said her mother, amazed. "I thought I saw pearls and diamonds coming out of your mouth. Where do they come from, daughter?" (It was the first time she had ever called her "daughter.") The poor child told her what had happened to her as simply as she could, but not without spilling out a great many diamonds.

"Indeed!" said the mother. "Then I must send *my* daughter. Look, Fanny, look what comes out of your sister's mouth when she talks. Wouldn't you like to have the same gift? All you have to do is to go and fetch water from the fountain. When a poor woman asks you for a drink, give her one very politely."

"Catch me going to the fountain," replied the rude girl.

"You must go," said her mother, "at once."

So off she went, grumbling all the way. She took the best silver flask in the house. Hardly had she reached the fountain, when she saw a magnificently dressed lady coming out of the wood. She came up and asked her for a drink. It was the same fairy who had appeared to her sister. But now she had taken on the form and clothing of a princess to see how far the girl's rudeness would go.

"Do you think I came all this way to give you a drink?" the rude, stuck-up girl said to her. "I suppose you think I brought this silver flask specially for you, madam. Get a drink from the fountain yourself if you want one."

"You are not very polite," replied the fairy without getting angry. "Well, then, because you are so unkind I will give you a gift. At each word you speak a snake or a toad will fall from your mouth."

As soon as her mother saw her, she cried out:

"Well, daughter?"

"Well, Mother?" replied the rude girl spitting out two snakes and two toads.

"Oh, heavens," cried the mother. "What's all this? It must be your sister's fault. I'll pay her out!"

She ran after her at once to beat her. But the poor girl ran away and hid in the forest nearby. The King's son passed by on his way back from hunting. Seeing how beautiful she was, he asked her what she was doing all alone and why she was crying.

"Alas, sir, my mother has driven me away from home."

The King's son saw five or six pearls and as many diamonds fall from her mouth. He asked her to tell him how it happened. So she told him the whole story. The King's son fell in love with her at once. Thinking that a gift like that was worth far more than any dowry that another girl might bring him, he took her back to his father's palace where he married her.

As for her sister, she made herself so hated that even her mother drove her away from home. After the poor wretch had wandered around without finding anyone to take her in, she lay down and died in a corner of the wood.

FIRST MORAL

Good manners are not easy
They need a little care,
But when we least expect it
Bring rewards both rich and rare.

SECOND MORAL

Brute force or bribes of diamonds
Bend others to your will,
But gentle words have greater power
And gain more conquests still.

The Master Cat or
Puss in Boots

A MILLER DIED leaving his three children his mill, his donkey and his cat. His estate was quickly shared. There was no need to call in lawyers. They would soon have used up all the little wealth that was left. The oldest son had the mill, the second had the donkey and the youngest only the cat. He could not get over having such a poor share.

"My brothers will be able to earn a good living if they work together," he said. "But once I've eaten my cat and made myself a muff from his fur, I'll have to starve to death."

The cat, who heard what he said although he pretended not to, said in a calm, serious voice:

"Don't worry, master. Just give me a sack and have a pair of boots made for me so that I can go through the bramblebushes, and you'll find that your share isn't as bad as you think."

The cat's master did not have much faith in what he said. But he had seen him do such extraordinary tricks to catch rats and mice, such as hanging upside down by his feet or hiding in the flour bin pretending to be dead, that he began to think the cat might be able to help him out of his misery.

As soon as the cat had what he asked, he pulled on his boots, slung his sack on his back, holding the strings with his paws, and went off to a warren where there were a great many rabbits. He put some bran and some thistles in the sack and lay down as if he were dead. Then he waited for a young rabbit, who was not used to the wiles of the world, to hop into his sack to eat what was in it.

Hardly had he lain down when the trick worked. A foolish young rabbit jumped into the sack and the Master Cat quickly pulled the strings tight and caught and killed him without mercy.

Proud of his catch, he went off to the King's palace and asked to speak to him. He was taken up to the King's chamber and, as he came in, he made a low bow and said:

"Sire, here is a wild rabbit that My Lord the Marquis of Carabas (that was the name he decided to give his master) has asked me to give you on his behalf."

"Tell your master," replied the King, "that I thank him and that he has given me great pleasure."

Next time he went and hid in a cornfield holding his sack open. When two partridges hopped in he pulled the strings tight and caught them both. Then he went to offer them to the King, just as he had done with the rabbit. The King again accepted the two partridges with pleasure and asked his men to give the cat some refreshment.

The cat went on like this for two or three months, taking the King game from his master's hunting. One day, when he knew the King was going for a drive along the riverbank with his daughter, the most beautiful princess in the world, he said to his master:

"If you follow my advice your fortune will be made. All you have to do is to bathe in the river at the place I'll show you. Leave the rest to me."

The Marquis of Carabas did as his cat said, without knowing what would come of it. While he was bathing the King came by, and the cat began to shout at the top of his voice:

"Help! Help! My Lord the Marquis of Carabas is drowning!"

At his cry the King put his head out of the carriage window. He recognized the cat that had brought him game so often and ordered his guards to hurry to the rescue of My Lord the Marquis of Carabas.

As they were pulling the poor Marquis out of the river, the cat came up to the carriage. He told the King that, while his master was bathing, some thieves had stolen all his clothes although he had shouted, "Stop thief!" with all his might. (The cunning cat had really hidden them under a big stone.)

The King at once ordered the officers of his wardrobe to go and fetch one of his finest suits for My Lord the Marquis of Carabas. The King treated him very kindly. The fine clothes he had been given set off his good looks so well (for he was handsome and well-built) that the King's daughter took a great liking to him. By the time the Marquis of Carabas had given her two or three respectful and tender glances, she had fallen madly in love with him.

The King insisted that he get into the carriage and continue the drive with them. The cat was delighted that his plan was beginning to succeed. He ran on ahead and when he met some farmers cutting the hay he said to them:

"My good haymakers, if you don't tell the King that the hay you are cutting belongs to My Lord the Marquis of Carabas, I'll have you all chopped up into mincemeat."

Of course the King asked the haymakers whose grass they were cutting.

"It belongs to My Lord the Marquis of Carabas," they all said in chorus, because they were frightened by the cat's threat.

"You have a fine property here," said the King to the Marquis of Carabas.

"As you see, Sire," replied the Marquis, "this meadow gives us a good crop every year."

The Master Cat, still running ahead, met some harvesters and said to them:

"My good harvesters, if you don't say that all these cornfields belong to My Lord the Marquis of Carabas, I'll have you all chopped up into mincemeat."

When the King came by a moment later, he wanted to know who owned all the cornfields he saw.

"They belong to My Lord the Marquis of Carabas," replied the harvesters, and the King again congratulated the Marquis. The cat went on ahead of the carriage saying the same thing to all the people he met. And the King was astonished at the huge property of the Marquis of Carabas.

At last the Master Cat reached a fine castle that belonged to an ogre. He was the richest ogre of all. All the land the King had driven through belonged to him. The cat, who had found out all about this ogre and what he could do, asked to speak to him. He said that he did not want to pass by his castle without paying him his respects.

The ogre received him as politely as an ogre can and asked him to sit down.

"They tell me," said the cat, "that you have the power of changing yourself into all kinds of animals. For instance, that you can turn yourself into a lion or an elephant."

"It's quite true," said the ogre gruffly. "Just to show you, I'll turn myself into a lion."

The cat was so scared at finding himself face to face with a lion that he rushed up the drainpipe onto the roof, not without some danger and difficulty because his boots were no good for walking on the tiles.

A little while later, when he saw that the ogre had turned back into his original shape, he came down and admitted that he'd had a bad fright.

"I was also told," said the cat, "though I can hardly believe it, that you have the power to change yourself into the shape of a tiny animal such as a rat or a mouse. I must admit that I think that's quite impossible."

"Impossible?" roared the ogre. "You'll see!"

Immediately he turned himself into a mouse that began to run across the floor. No sooner had the cat spotted it than he pounced on it and ate it up.

Meanwhile the King, who was passing by the ogre's fine castle, wanted to visit it. The cat heard the noise of the carriage on the drawbridge and ran out to say to the King:

"Welcome, Your Majesty, to the castle of My Lord the Marquis of Carabas."

"What, My Lord Marquis," said the King, "is this castle yours too? Nothing could be more beautiful than this courtyard and the buildings round it. May we see inside, please?"

The Marquis gave his arm to the young Princess and, following the King, they went up into the great hall. There they found a magnificent banquet that the ogre had made ready for his friends who were coming to see him that day. They had not dared to come in when they heard that the King was there.

The King was delighted with all the fine qualities of My Lord the Marquis of Carabas. As for his daughter, she was madly in love with him. Seeing all the riches he possessed, the King said, after he'd drunk five or six glasses of wine:

"My Lord Marquis, say the word and you will become my son-in-law."

Making a low bow, the Marquis accepted the honor that the King proposed. That very same day he married the Princess. The cat became a great Lord and, from then on, only ran after mice when he wanted to amuse himself.

FIRST MORAL

Some people have the luck to own
A fortune that's been handed down
The family line from father to son.
But those who have to make their way
Will find the truth of what I say—
Cunning and hard work always pay.

SECOND MORAL

If a miller's son, a mere upstart,
Can quickly win a princess's heart
And make her gaze with lovelorn eyes,
It means that fine clothes and good looks
And youth will serve as splendid hooks
To catch and keep so fair a prize.

Cinderella or
The Little Glass Slipper

ONCE UPON A TIME there was a nobleman who took for his second wife the proudest and haughtiest woman you have ever seen. She had two daughters who were just like her. On his side, the husband had a young daughter who was as sweet and kind as could be. She got this from her mother who had been one of the loveliest people in the world.

No sooner was the wedding over than the stepmother began to show her bad temper. She could not bear to see the young girl's good nature, it made her own daughters seem even more hateful. So she made her do all the rough work of the house. She had to wash the dishes and clean the stairs, sweep Madam's room and her daughters' too. She slept right at the top of the house in an attic on a hard straw mattress, while her sisters' rooms had fine, polished floors. They had beds in the latest style and mirrors in which they could see themselves from head to foot. The poor girl put up with it all patiently and didn't dare complain to her father. He would only have scolded her, because he was completely under his wife's thumb.

When she had finished her work, she used to go and sit down in the chimney corner among the cinders. Because of this, they used to call her Cinderbottom. But her younger stepsister, who was not so rude as her sister, called her Cinderella. In spite of all this, Cinderella in her ragged clothes was a hundred times more beautiful than her sisters in their finery.

One day the King's son gave a ball, to which all the grand people were invited. Our two young ladies got invitations because they were quite well known round about. So there they were, very pleased with themselves and very busy choosing which dress and which hairstyle would suit them best. All this made even more work for Cinderella. For it was she who had to iron her sisters' underwear and

starch their cuffs. They talked about nothing else but what they would wear.

"I shall wear my red velvet gown," said the eldest, "and my collar of English lace."

"I'll wear my ordinary skirt," said the youngest, "but to make up for it I'll put on my gold-embroidered cape and my diamond brooch. They are rather special."

They sent for the best hairdresser to curl their hair in double ringlets and they bought beauty spots for their cheeks from the best shop. They called Cinderella to ask what she thought because she had good taste. Cinderella gave them the best possible advice. She even offered to arrange their hair for them and they were very pleased.

While she was brushing their hair, they said to her:

"Cinderella, wouldn't you like to go to the ball?"

"Oh dear, you're making fun of me. It wouldn't do for me at all."

"You're quite right. People would laugh if they saw a Cinderbottom at the ball."

Anyone else but Cinderella would have tangled their hair. But she was so good-natured that she brushed it beautifully. For nearly two days they were so excited that they ate next to nothing. They broke more than a dozen laces trying to pull their stays tighter to make their waists look smaller. And they were always in front of their mirrors.

At last the great day arrived. Off they went and Cinderella watched them go as long as she could. As soon as they were out of sight she began to cry. When her godmother saw her in tears she asked what was the matter.

"If only I . . . if only I could . . ." She was crying so much that she could not go on.

Her godmother, who was a fairy, said:

"You'd like to go to the ball, isn't that it?"

"Alas, yes," said Cinderella.

"Very well," said her godmother, "if you're good, I'll arrange it."

She took her to her room and said:

"Go into the garden and bring me a pumpkin."

Cinderella went at once to pick the best she could find. She took it back to her godmother but she could not see how this pumpkin would get her to the ball. Her godmother hollowed it out, leaving only the rind. Then she touched it with her wand and the pumpkin turned into a beautiful golden coach.

Next she went and looked in the mousetrap where she found six mice still alive. She told Cinderella to raise the door of the trap a little and, as each mouse came out, she tapped it with her wand and the mouse changed into a fine horse. They made a team of six horses of dappled gray.

36

While she was wondering how to make a coachman, Cinderella said:

"I'll go and see if there's a rat in the rattrap. We could turn him into a coachman."

"You're right," said her godmother. "Run and see." Cinderella brought her the rattrap which had three big rats in it. The fairy chose the one with the longest whiskers. As soon as she touched him he turned into a fat coachman with the finest mustache you've ever seen.

Next she said:

"Go into the garden. You'll find six lizards behind the watering can. Bring them to me."

As soon as she had brought them her godmother turned them into six footmen. They climbed up behind the coach and stood there in their striped livery, as if they had been doing it all their lives.

Then the fairy said to Cinderella:

"Well, then, everything's ready to go to the ball. Aren't you pleased?"

"Yes. But must I go like this, in my ugly clothes?"

Her godmother had only to touch her with her wand for her clothes to be changed into a dress of gold and silver cloth, all sparkling with precious stones. Then she gave her a pair of glass slippers, the most beautiful in all the world. As soon as she was ready she got into the coach. Then her godmother warned her above all not to stay out after midnight. She told her that if she stayed at the ball a moment longer, her coach would turn back into a pumpkin, her horses into mice, her footmen into lizards and her clothes would turn back into rags again.

She promised her godmother that she would leave the ball before midnight. Then off she went, beside herself with joy. The King's son, on hearing that a grand princess that no one knew was just arriving, ran out to welcome her. He handed her down from the coach and led her into the hall where everyone was. A sudden silence fell. They all stopped dancing. The violins ceased to play. Everyone stood spellbound by the great beauty of this unknown princess. You could hear a low murmur:

"Oh! How beautiful she is!"

The King himself, old as he was, couldn't stop looking at her and whispered to the Queen that he had not seen so beautiful and charming a person for a long time. All the ladies were studying her hair and her clothes so that they could copy them the next day, if they could find fine enough material and skillful enough dressmakers.

The King's son put her in the place of honor and then led her out to dance. She danced with such grace that they admired her even more. A magnificent supper was brought in, but the young Prince could not eat anything because he was so

busy gazing at her. She went and sat next to her sisters and gave them some of the oranges and lemons that the Prince had given her. They were amazed, because they did not recognize her at all.

As they were talking, Cinderella heard the clock strike a quarter to twelve—she made a low curtesy to the company and left as quickly as she could. As soon as she got back home, she went to find her godmother. She thanked her and asked if she could go to the ball again the next night, for the King's son had begged her to come back. While she was busy telling her godmother all the things that had happened at the ball, her two sisters knocked on the door. Cinderella went to open it.

"How late you are coming back," she said to them, yawning and rubbing her eyes as if she had just waked up. Really she hadn't felt at all sleepy since she left them.

"If you had been at the ball," said one of her sisters, "you wouldn't have felt like yawning. There was the most beautiful princess there, the most beautiful you could hope to see. She was very polite to us. She gave us oranges and lemons."

Cinderella was delighted. She asked them the name of the princess, but they replied that no one knew her. They said that the King's son was very troubled about it and would give anything in the world to know who she was. Cinderella smiled and said to them:

"Was she really so beautiful? How lucky you are. Couldn't I see her too? Please, Miss Javotte, would you lend me the yellow dress you wear for every day?"

"Really," said Miss Javotte. "Do you think I would? Lend my dress to a dirty Cinderbottom like you? I'd be crazy."

Cinderella was expecting her to refuse and she was glad. It would have been very awkward if her sister had really lent her a dress.

The next day the two sisters went to the ball and so did Cinderella. But this time she was even more splendidly dressed than before. The King's son was always by her side and paid her compliments the whole evening. The young girl was enjoying herself so much that she quite forgot what her godmother had said. So much so that she heard the first stroke of midnight chiming when she thought it was only eleven o'clock. She got up and fled away as lightly as a deer. The Prince followed her but he could not catch her up. One of her glass slippers fell off, and the Prince picked it up carefully.

Cinderella arrived home quite out of breath. She had no coach, no footmen and was wearing her old rags. Nothing remained of all her fine things, except one little glass slipper, the twin of the one she had dropped. The guards at the palace gate were asked if they had seen a princess leaving. They said they had seen no one go out at all except a young girl, very poorly dressed, more like a peasant than a young lady.

When her two sisters came back from the ball, Cinderella asked them if they had enjoyed themselves again and if the beautiful lady had been there. They said yes, but she had fled away at the stroke of midnight, so swiftly that she lost one of her little glass slippers, the prettiest in the world. The Prince had picked it up and had gazed at it all the rest of the ball. There was no doubt he was very much in love with the beautiful person who owned the little slipper.

They were telling the truth. A few days later the King's son had it proclaimed to the sound of trumpets that he would marry the girl whose foot exactly fitted the slipper. First they tried it on various princesses, then on duchesses and on all the ladies of the court, but all in vain. Then it was brought to the two sisters. They did their best to squeeze their feet into the slipper but they could not manage it. Cinderella was watching them and, when she recognized her own slipper, she said, laughing:

"Let me see if it fits me."

Her sisters began to mock and tease her. But the gentleman who was trying on the slipper looked closely at Cinderella. Seeing that she was very beautiful, he said that she was quite right. His orders were to try it on every girl. He made Cinderella sit down and, as he slid her foot into the slipper, he saw that it went on easily and fitted her like a glove. Her two sisters' astonishment was great and it grew even greater when Cinderella pulled the other little slipper out of her pocket and put it on her other foot. At that moment her godmother appeared and touched Cinderella's clothes with her wand, making them even more magnificent than before.

Then the two sisters recognized her as the beautiful princess they had seen at the ball. They threw themselves at her feet to beg her forgiveness for all the unkind things they had done to her. Cinderella raised them up and kissed them, saying that she forgave them with all her heart, and begged them to love her always. She was taken to the Prince in the fine clothes she was wearing. He thought her even more beautiful than before and, a few days later, he married her. Cinderella was as kind as she was beautiful. She brought her two sisters to live in the palace and married them the same day to two grand noblemen of the court.

FIRST MORAL

Beauty in girls is something rare
And people cannot help but stare.
But loving kindness brings such grace
It's worth more than a pretty face.

Her godmother taught Cinderella
All her charm, watched over her,
And made her fit to be a queen.
(The moral's easy to be seen.)

So, girls, forget about your hair
For that won't make you loved, I fear.
The fairies' gift is a loving heart.
If you have that you need no art.

SECOND MORAL

No doubt it's very lucky
To be born with lots of sense,
To be brave and be witty
To be clever and not dense.
But all these things won't take you far
Unless you have as well
A real fairy godmother
To work a magic spell.

Ricky with the Tuft

Once upon a time there was a Queen who gave birth to a son who was so ugly and deformed that people wondered if he was human. A fairy, who was there at his birth, told them not to worry because he would be so intelligent that he was sure to be loved. She also said that the gift she had made him would give him the power to make the person he loved best as intelligent as he was himself.

This comforted the poor Queen a little for she was very upset at bringing such an ugly brat into the world. Sure enough, as soon as he could talk he said so many witty things and was so charming in all his ways that everyone was delighted with him. I forgot to say that he came into the world with a little tuft of hair on his head, so he was called Ricky with the Tuft—Ricky was a family name.

After seven or eight years, the Queen of a neighboring kingdom gave birth to two daughters. The first to be born was as beautiful as the day. The Queen was so overjoyed that they thought her excitement might do her some harm. The same fairy, who had helped at the birth of Ricky of the Tuft, was there. To calm the Queen she declared that the little Princess would have no brains at all and would be as stupid as she was beautiful. This upset the Queen very much. But her grief was greater when, a few moments later, she gave birth to a second daughter who was extremely ugly.

"Don't get so upset, madam," said the fairy. "To make up for it, your daughter will be so clever that people will hardly notice she isn't beautiful."

"Praise God for that!" replied the Queen. "But is there no way of giving a little intelligence to the elder one, who is so beautiful?"

"I can do nothing about her intelligence, madam," said the fairy. "But I can do something to do with her beauty. So, as there is nothing I would not do to please you, I will give her the power to make the person she likes best beautiful."

As these two princesses grew up, so their gifts grew with them. People talked

44

of nothing but the beauty of the eldest and the intelligence of the youngest. But their faults grew even greater as well. The youngest became uglier and uglier, and the eldest more and more stupid every day. Either she gave no answer when people spoke to her or she said something silly. Besides this, she was so clumsy that she could not put four china bowls on the mantelpiece without breaking one of them or drink a glass of water without spilling half of it all down her clothes.

Although it's a great asset for a young girl to be beautiful, even so the youngest was always more popular than her sister when they went out. At first people clustered round to admire the beautiful girl, but very soon they moved over to the clever one to listen to all the witty things she had to say. After a quarter of an hour the eldest had no one near her at all. Everyone was gathered round the younger sister. Although she was stupid the elder girl couldn't help noticing. She would gladly have given all her beauty for half her sister's wit. Besides this, the Queen, for all her good sense, couldn't help scolding her sometimes for her stupidity. And this made the poor Princess sadder than ever.

One day, when she had gone off into the woods thinking sadly about her misfortune, she saw a little man coming toward her. He was very ugly but most magnificently dressed. It was the young Prince Ricky with the Tuft. He had fallen in love with the portraits of her that were to be seen in many distant places. So much so, that he had left his father's kingdom in the hope of meeting her and talking to her. Delighted at finding her all alone, he came up to her with great respect and courtesy. He paid her all the usual compliments and then, noticing how sad she looked, he said:

"I don't understand, madam, how someone as beautiful as you are can be as sad as you seem to be. Although I can boast of having seen a great many beautiful girls, I must say that I've never seen anyone nearly as beautiful as you."

"You flatter me, sir," replied the Princess, and stopped there.

"Beauty," went on Ricky with the Tuft, "is such a great asset that it surpasses any other. I don't understand how anyone who possesses it could be upset by anything."

"I would much rather be as ugly as you," said the Princess, "and have some brains, than be as beautiful and stupid as I am."

"There is nothing, madam, that shows intelligence more clearly than the belief that one has none. The more intelligent a person the less intelligent they think they are."

"I don't know about that," said the Princess, "but I do know that I'm very stupid and that's why I'm so unhappy."

"If that's all that worries you, madam, I can easily put an end to your grief."

"How would you do that?" asked the Princess.

"I have the power," said Ricky with the Tuft, "to make the person I love best

as intelligent as anyone could be. As you, madam, are that person, you have only to say that you are willing to marry me to have all the brains you could want."

The Princess was quite amazed and made no answer.

"I see," went on Ricky with the Tuft, "that you find my proposal hard to accept and I'm not surprised. But I'll give you a whole year to make up your mind."

The Princess had so little brains and, at the same time, so longed to have some, that she imagined the end of the year would never come. So she accepted his suggestion. No sooner had she promised Ricky with the Tuft that she would marry him one year from that day, than she felt herself becoming quite different. She found it easy to say whatever she wanted as wittily and naturally as she pleased. Straight away she began to have a long amusing conversation with Ricky with the Tuft. She babbled away so eloquently that he was afraid he had given her more brains than he had himself.

When she got back to the palace, no one knew what to make of the sudden and amazing change in her. Now she was as sensible and witty in her talk as she had been foolish before. The whole court was overjoyed. Only her younger sister was not pleased. Now she no longer had the advantage of being more intelligent, she seemed a most unattractive lump beside her beautiful sister.

The King listened to her advice. He sometimes even held his council meetings in her rooms. As soon as the rumor of her transformation was spread abroad, all the young princes of the neighboring kingdoms did their best to woo her love. Nearly all of them asked for her hand in marriage. But she did not find any one of them intelligent enough for her, and she listened to them all without accepting any.

Then at last one came along who was so powerful, so rich, so intelligent and so handsome that she could not help liking him. When her father noticed it, he told her that it was up to her to choose her own husband. She had only to say whom she preferred. But the more intelligent one is, the harder it is to make up one's mind on such matters. So she thanked her father and asked him to give her time to think it over.

Quite by chance she went walking in the same wood where she had met Ricky with the Tuft to think quietly about what she should do.

While she was walking along, deep in thought, she heard a muffled noise coming from under the ground as if people were very busy hurrying to and fro. Listening more carefully, she heard someone say:

"Bring me that stewpot."

And another: "Give me that saucepan."

And another: "Put more wood on the fire."

At the same moment the ground opened and at her feet she saw a huge kitchen full of cooks, kitchen boys and all the servants necessary to prepare a huge banquet. A row of twenty or thirty cooks came marching into a clearing in the wood where they took up their places round a very long table. With long forks in their hands and cook's hats on their heads they began to work together, singing all the while.

The Princess was amazed at this sight and asked them whom they were working for.

"Why, madam," replied the leader, "for Prince Ricky with the Tuft. It's his wedding day tomorrow."

The Princess was more surprised than ever. Suddenly she remembered that it was exactly a year to the day since she had promised to marry Prince Ricky with the Tuft. She thought she would faint. What had made her forget was that when she made her promise she had been stupid. With the new mind that the Prince had given her, all her old foolish ways had been forgotten.

She had not gone thirty paces more on her walk when Ricky with the Tuft appeared before her. He was magnificently dressed, like a prince on the way to his wedding.

"You see me here, madam," said he, "to keep my promise. And I'm sure that you have come here to keep yours."

"I must tell you frankly," replied the Princess, "that I haven't yet made up my mind. And I'm afraid I may never be able to decide in the way you wish."

"You astonish me, madam," said Ricky with the Tuft.

"I'm sure I do," said the Princess, "and if I was dealing with some rough fellow without any intelligence, I should be very embarrassed. 'A princess always keeps her word,' he would say, 'and you must marry me because you promised you would.' But, as I'm speaking to the most intelligent man in the world, I'm sure he will be reasonable. You know that even when I was stupid I could not make up my mind to marry you. And now you've made me so clever that I'm even more choosy about people than I was before, how do you expect me to make a decision that I couldn't make then? If you really meant to marry me, you made a great mistake in taking away my stupidity and making me see things more clearly than I did before."

"If a stupid man," replied Ricky with the Tuft, "would behave as you described and reproach you for not keeping your word, why would you expect me, madam, to behave any differently over something on which all my life's happiness depends? Is it reasonable that intelligent people should be worse off than stupid ones? Let us get to the point, please. Apart from my ugliness, is there anything else about me that you dislike? Are you dissatisfied with my breeding, my wit, my character or my manners?"

48

"Not at all," replied the Princess, "I like all those things in you."

"If that's the case," went on Ricky with the Tuft, "I shall be happy, because you can make me the most lovable of men."

"How can that be?" said the Princess.

"It will happen," replied Ricky with the Tuft, "if you like me enough to wish it. You see, madam, the same fairy who gave me the gift of making the person I loved intelligent, also gave you the power to make the person you loved good-looking."

"If that's the case," said the Princess, "I wish with all my heart for you to become the most handsome prince in all the world. I wish it to the utmost of my power."

No sooner had the Princess said these words, than Ricky with the Tuft became in her eyes the handsomest, most attractive and lovable man in all the world. Some people say that it wasn't the fairy's magic that did the trick, but love alone. They say that when the Princess thought about the persistence of her lover, his tact and all his good qualities of mind and spirit, she no longer saw his misshapen body and the ugliness of his face. The lump on his back seemed only part of his broad shoulders. Whereas before she thought he limped very badly, now she saw only a slight sway that fascinated her. They say, too, that his cross-eyes seemed to her to shine and their squint now seemed to her to show intense love. Even his big, red nose seemed soldierly and heroic.

FIRST MORAL

The story that you've read today
Is based on truth not fantasy.
For love finds beauty everywhere
And makes both mind and body fair.

SECOND MORAL

Whatever beauty Nature gives at birth,
Sweet, rosy cheeks, a handsome face and form
That all our art could never imitate,
Are still not half such powerful attractions
As those rare qualities of mind and soul
That no one knows till love discovers them.

Tom Thumb

ONCE UPON A TIME there was a woodcutter and his wife who had seven children, all boys. The eldest was only ten, and the youngest was seven. It may seem surprising that the woodcutter had so many children in so short a time. But his wife was a quick worker and always had at least two children at once.

They were very poor and their seven children were a great burden to them because none of them could earn his living. What worried them even more was that the youngest child was very delicate and never spoke. They thought he was stupid but it was really a sign of his sweet nature. He was tiny. When he was born he was no bigger than a thumb, so they called him Tom Thumb.

The poor child was the butt of all the household. He was always in the wrong. Yet he was the wisest and cleverest of all the brothers. He spoke little, but he noticed everything.

It happened that there was a particularly hard year. The famine was so great that these poor people decided to get rid of their children. One evening, when the children were in bed and the woodcutter was sitting with his wife beside the fire, he said to her with an aching heart:

"You can see that we can no longer feed our children. I cannot bear to watch them die of hunger before my own eyes, so I have decided to take them to the wood tomorrow and lose them. It will be easy. While they're busy picking up sticks we can slip away without them noticing."

"Oh," cried the woodcutter's wife, "how could you bear to take your own children into the wood to get lost?"

Her husband pointed out their great poverty, but she would not agree. She was poor but, after all, she was their mother. But when she realized how painful it would be for her to see them die of hunger, she agreed and went weeping to bed.

Tom Thumb overheard everything they were saying. He had heard them talking about something serious from his own bed, so he got up quietly and slid under his father's stool, where he could listen without being seen. He went back to bed and stayed awake all the rest of the night thinking what he should do. Next morning he got up early and went down to the edge of the stream where he filled his pockets with little white pebbles. Then he came back to the house. Off they all went, and Tom Thumb said nothing to his brothers about what he knew.

They reached a dense part of the forest where they could not see each other at a few yards distance. The woodcutter began to cut wood and his children picked up sticks for firewood. When the father and mother saw that they were busy working, they slipped away unnoticed and then hurried off down a side path.

As soon as the children found themselves alone they began to shout and cry with all their might. Tom Thumb let them cry because he knew how to get back to the house. On the way he had dropped the little white pebbles that he had in his pockets all along the road. So he said to them:

"Don't be afraid, brothers. My father and mother have left us here, but I'll take you back home again. Just follow me."

They followed him and he led them all the way home by the same road that they had taken into the forest. When they reached the house at first they did not dare go in. They pressed close to the door to hear what their father and mother were saying.

At the very moment when the woodcutter and his wife had reached home, the Lord of the Manor had sent them ten crowns. He had owed them the money for a long time, and they had given up hope of getting it. This money saved their lives because they were dying of hunger. The woodcutter at once sent his wife to the butcher. Because they had eaten nothing for a long time, she bought three times as much meat as she needed for two people's supper. When they were full up, the wife said:

"Alas, where are our poor children now? They could have a good meal from what's left over. It was you, William, who wanted to lose them. I told you we'd be sorry. What are they doing now in the forest? Alas, dear God, perhaps the wolves have eaten them! How cruel you were to abandon your children like that!"

In the end the woodcutter lost his temper because she said over twenty times that they would be sorry for what they had done and that she'd told him so. He threatened to beat her if she wouldn't keep quiet. He was probably just as upset about it as his wife, but she was driving him crazy. He was one of those men who want women to talk sense but can't bear for them to be always in the right.

The woodcutter's wife was in tears:

"Alas, where are my children now, my poor, poor children?"

She said it so loudly that the children, who were listening at the door, heard her and began to shout all together:

"Here we are. Here we are!"

She ran to open the door for them, and said as she hugged them:

"I'm so pleased to see you, dear children! How tired you are! How hungry you are! And you, Peter, you're covered with mud! Come here and let me clean you up."

Peter was her eldest son. She loved him more than the others because he had reddish hair and hers was a bit red too.

They sat down at the table and ate with an appetite that delighted their father and mother. All speaking at once, they told them how frightened they had been in the forest. Their parents were overjoyed to have their children back again, and their joy lasted as long as the ten crowns did. But, as soon as the money was all spent, they slipped back into their old poverty and made up their minds to lose the children again. In order to make no mistake this time, they decided to take them much farther into the forest.

They could not talk about it without being overheard by Tom Thumb, who thought he could get out of the forest the same way as before. But although he got up very early in the morning to go and collect pebbles, he could not manage it because he found the door of the house locked and bolted. He did not know what to do until the woodcutter's wife gave them each a bit of bread for breakfast. Then he had the idea of using the bread instead of pebbles and throwing down crumbs all along the path. So he hid the bread in his pocket.

The father and mother led them into the thickest and darkest part of the forest. Once there, they tricked them again and left them there. Tom Thumb was not worried because he thought he could easily find the way back by means of the bread that he had scattered as he passed. But he was very surprised when he couldn't find a single crumb. The birds had come and eaten it all.

So there they were, very upset. The more they walked, the deeper they went into the forest. Night came and a strong wind blew up that filled them with terror. All around them they thought they heard wolves howling and coming to eat them up. They hardly dared to speak or look back. Then the rain came down, soaking them to the skin. At every step they slipped and fell in the mud, struggling up again with their hands all sticky with grime.

Tom Thumb climbed up to the top of a tree to see if he could see anything. Looking round on all sides, he saw a little light like a candle, far away the other side of the forest. When he came down from the tree he could not see it any more. He was very upset, but he led his brothers in the direction where he had last seen it and, as they came out of the wood, they caught sight of it again.

At last they reached the house where the candle was burning, not without great fear because every time the path dipped down they lost sight of the light. They knocked on the door and a kind woman opened it. She asked them what they wanted. Tom Thumb told her that they were poor children lost in the forest and asked her to let them have a bed for pity's sake. When the woman saw how charming they all were she began to cry and said:

"Alas, poor children, what a place to come to! Don't you know that this house belongs to an ogre who eats little children?"

"Alas, madam," replied Tom Thumb, shaking with fear, like all his brothers, "what shall we do? The wolves are sure to eat us up tonight if you don't give us shelter. If we have to be eaten, we'd rather be eaten by your Lord Ogre. Perhaps he will take pity on us if you beg him to."

The ogre's wife thought she could hide them from her husband till the next morning. So she let them come in and warm themselves beside the fire, where a whole sheep was roasting on the spit for the ogre's supper.

Just as they were getting warm they heard a knocking on the door. It was the ogre coming back. The wife quickly hid them under the bed and went to open the door. The ogre asked if supper was ready and the wine served, and straight-away he sat down at the table. The mutton was still half raw, but he liked it all the better. He began to sniff, first on this side then on that, saying that he could smell human flesh.

"It must be the veal I was preparing that you can smell," said his wife.

"I smell human flesh, I tell you," said the ogre, looking crossly at his wife. "There's something going on here that I don't know about."

As he said this, he got up from the table and went straight to the bed.

"Aha!" he said. "I see your tricks, you wicked woman. I don't know why I don't eat you too! You're lucky to be such a tough old creature. These children will do nicely to feed those three ogre friends of mine who are coming to see me one day soon."

He pulled them out from under the bed, one after another. The poor children went down on their knees to beg for mercy. But he was the cruelest of all the ogres. Far from having pity on them, he was already feasting on them with his eyes and he told his wife they would make tasty morsels if she cooked them with a good sauce.

He went to get a huge knife and came toward the children sharpening it on a long stone that he held in his left hand. He had already seized one of them when his wife said:

"What are you doing at this time of night? Won't you have plenty of time tomorrow?"

"Be quiet," said the ogre, "the longer they hang, the more tender they will be."

"But you've still got a lot of meat left," said his wife. "There's a calf, two sheep and half a pig."

"You're right," said the ogre. "Give them plenty of food to keep them fat and put them to bed."

The kind woman was delighted and gave them a good supper. But they were much too frightened to eat. As for the ogre, he went back to his wine, pleased to have such fine fare to give his friends. He drank a dozen more glasses than usual. It went to his head and he had to go to bed.

The ogre had seven daughters who were still only children. These young ogresses had lovely pink cheeks because they ate human flesh like their father. But they had round, gray eyes, hooked noses and big mouths with long, sharp teeth with gaps between them. They were not yet very wicked, but they soon would be. Already they bit babies to suck their blood.

They had been put to bed early and all seven of them were lying in one big bed, each with a gold crown on her head. In the same room there was another bed of equal size. And in this bed the ogre's wife put the seven little boys to sleep. After that she went and lay down next to her husband.

Tom Thumb noticed that the ogre's daughters had gold crowns on their heads. Fearing that the ogre might be sorry he had not cut their throats that evening, he got up in the middle of the night and took off his brothers' caps and his own. Then he put them gently on the heads of the ogre's seven daughters, after he had put their gold crowns on his brothers' heads and his own. In this way the ogre would take them for his daughters and would think his daughters were the boys he wanted to kill.

It happened just as he had thought. At midnight the ogre woke up and wished he had not put off till the next day what he could have done that evening. So he leaped out of bed and, seizing his big knife, he said:

"Let's see how the little monkeys are getting on. I won't be put off a second time."

He groped his way to his daughters' room and went up to the boys' bed. They were all asleep, except for Tom Thumb, who was terrified when he felt the ogre's hand passing over his head as it had passed over his brothers. When the ogre felt the gold crowns he said:

"What a stupid thing I was going to do! I must have drunk too much last night."

Next he went over to his daughters' bed and, feeling the boys' caps, he said:

"Aha! Here they are, the rascals. Let's get on with the job."

As he said this he cut the throats of his seven daughters at one blow. Very pleased with what he had done, he went and lay down again beside his wife.

As soon as Tom Thumb heard the ogre snoring, he woke up his brothers and told them to dress quickly and follow him. They crept down to the garden and scrambled over the wall. They ran almost all night, trembling with fear, without knowing where they were going.

When the ogre woke up he said to his wife:

"Go upstairs and dress those little monkeys that came last night."

The ogress was amazed at her husband's kindness. She thought he meant her to dress them in their clothes. She did not think of the other meaning of "dressing." So up she went and was horrified to find her seven daughters swimming in blood with their throats cut.

She began by fainting (which is what nearly all women do in such circumstances). The ogre, thinking that his wife was taking too long over the job he had given her, went upstairs to help her. He was as amazed as his wife when he saw the terrible sight.

"What have I done?" he shouted. "I'll pay the little devils out for this straight away."

He threw a jug of water over his wife to revive her and said:

"Quick, fetch me my seven-league boots so that I can catch them."

Off he went over the countryside. After he had looked all over the place, at last he came to the road the poor children were walking along, not a hundred yards from their father's house. They saw the ogre leaping from mountaintop to mountaintop, crossing rivers as easily as if they were streams. Tom Thumb saw a hollow rock nearby and hid his six brothers and himself under it, peeping out to see what the ogre was doing. The ogre was exhausted after his long, fruitless journey (because seven-league boots are very tiring to wear). He wanted to have a rest and, quite by chance, he sat down on the rock under which the boys were hiding.

As he was very tired, he soon fell asleep and began to snore so dreadfully that the poor children were just as frightened as they had been when he was holding his huge knife ready to cut their throats. Tom Thumb was not so afraid. He told his brothers to run home while the ogre was sleeping and not to worry about him. They did what he said and quickly reached home.

Tom Thumb went up to the ogre, gently pulled off his boots and put them on himself. The boots were very wide and long but, as they were magic, they had the power of getting bigger or smaller according to the leg that was wearing them. So they fitted Tom Thumb's legs as if they had been made for him.

He went straight to the ogre's house where he found his wife weeping beside her daughters.

"Your husband is in great danger," Tom Thumb said to her. "He has been captured by a gang of robbers who have sworn to kill him unless he gives them all his gold and silver. Just as they were holding a dagger to his throat, he saw me

and begged me to come and warn you of his plight. He wants you to give me all the treasure he has. Keep nothing back because otherwise they will kill him without mercy. As there was no time to lose, he made me wear his seven-league boots. I put them on to get here more quickly and to show that I'm not a trickster."

The good woman was very frightened and at once gave him all she had, because the ogre was a good husband although he ate little children. Tom Thumb, weighed down with all the ogre's riches, went back to his father's house where he was welcomed with great joy.

There are some people who don't agree with the last part of this story and who say that Tom Thumb did not rob the ogre. They say he did not mind taking the seven-league boots because the ogre used them for chasing little children. These people claim to have it from a good source and even to have eaten and drunk in the woodcutter's house.

They say that when Tom Thumb had put on the ogre's boots he went straight to court where he knew they were worried about the army that was two hundred leagues from there. They wanted to know the result of a battle that had been fought. He went to the King, they say, and promised to bring him news of the army before nightfall, if he wished. The King promised him a large sum of money if he succeeded. Tom Thumb brought back news that same evening and, once this first exploit had made him known, he could earn what he wanted. For the King paid him well to carry his orders to the army, and a great many ladies gave him whatever he asked in order to have news of their lovers. That brought him in most profit. There were also some wives who gave him letters for their husbands. But they paid so badly, and there was so little in it, that he did not bother to take account of what he earned in this way.

After he had worked as a courier for some time and saved up a great deal of money, he went back to his father's house. You can hardly imagine what joy there was to see him again. He supported the whole family. He arranged jobs for his father and his brothers. In this way he got them all established and made sure of his own place at court at the same time.

MORAL

To have a lot of children is no sorrow
If they are tall and strong and handsome too,
And give delight to all who look at them.
But if one happens to be small and weak,
Then he is sure to be despised and teased.
And yet it may be this tiny fellow,
Despite his size, will make the family's fortune.

The Sleeping Beauty
in the Wood

ONCE UPON A TIME there lived a King and Queen who were sad because they had no children, more sad than words can tell. They went to all the magic springs in the world. They made vows, pilgrimages and humble prayers, but nothing happened. Then at last the Queen grew fat and gave birth to a daughter. There was a grand christening. For her godmothers, the little Princess had all the fairies that could be found in that country (they found seven), so that each one of them would make her a gift—the custom in those days—so the Princess would be perfect in every way.

After the christening ceremony, everyone came back to the King's palace where there was a great banquet for the fairies. The table was laid magnificently. In front of each of them was a casket of pure gold in which was a spoon, a fork and a knife of fine gold decorated with diamonds and rubies. But just as they were taking their places at the table, an old fairy came in who had not been invited because she had not left her tower for more than fifty years. People thought she was dead or bewitched. The King had a place laid for her, but it was impossible to give her a casket of pure gold like the others. Only seven had been made for the seven fairies. The old fairy thought she was being scorned and muttered curses under her breath. One of the young fairies, who was sitting nearby, heard her. Thinking that she might make the little Princess some spiteful gift, she hid herself behind the tapestry when they got up from the table. In this way she would be the last to speak and she might be able to make up for any harm the old fairy might do.

Meanwhile the fairies began to make their gifts to the Princess. The gift of the youngest was that she would be the most beautiful person in the world. The next, that she would have the spirit of an angel. The third, that she would do everything with wonderful grace. The fourth, that she would dance beautifully. The fifth,

that she would sing like a nightingale. The sixth, that she would play all kinds of musical instruments to perfection. When the old fairy's turn came, shaking with spite not old age, she said that the Princess would prick her hand with a spindle and that she would die from it.

This terrible gift made everyone tremble. There was no one who did not weep. At this moment, the young fairy came out from behind the tapestry and in a loud voice she spoke these words:

"Take comfort, King and Queen, your daughter will not die. It is true that I am not powerful enough to undo all that the old fairy has done. The Princess will prick her hand with a spindle but, instead of dying from it, she will only fall into a deep sleep that will last a hundred years. At the end of that time a King's son will come to wake her up."

Hoping to avoid the misfortune that the old fairy had foretold, the King published an edict forbidding people to spin or to have a spindle in their house, on pain of death.

Fifteen or sixteen years later when the King and Queen were away at one of their summer palaces, it happened that the young Princess was playing about in the castle one day. As she climbed higher and higher from room to room, she came to a little attic at the top of the castle keep, where a dear old woman was spinning with her distaff. This old woman had never heard of the laws the King had made against spinning.

"What are you doing, old lady?" asked the Princess.

"I am spinning, my sweet child," replied the old lady, who did not know who she was.

"Oh, how pretty it looks," said the Princess. "How do you do it? Let me see if I can do it as well as you."

Because she was too quick and a little thoughtless and, besides, because the fairy's decree had foretold it, no sooner had she taken the spindle than she pricked her hand and fell down in a trance.

The old lady was greatly upset and called out for help. People came running from all sides. They threw water on the Princess's face, they untied her bodice, they rubbed her hands, they massaged her forehead with lavender water, but nothing would make her come around.

Then the King, who had returned and come up to see what the noise was all about, remembered the fairy's prophecy. Realizing that this had to happen because the fairies had said so, he ordered the Princess to be taken to the most beautiful room in the palace and put on a bed embroidered with gold and silver. You would have thought her an angel, she was so beautiful. Her trance had not faded the lovely color of her complexion. Her cheeks were rosy and her lips were like coral. Her eyes were shut, but you could hear her breathing very gently which showed

64

she was not dead. The King commanded that she should be left to sleep in peace until the time should come for her to wake up.

When the accident happened to the Princess, the good fairy, who had saved her life by condemning her to sleep for a hundred years, was in the Kingdom of Mataquin, twelve thousand leagues away. But she was told about it at once by a little dwarf who had a pair of seven-league boots. (Those are boots that can make you go seven leagues in one step.) The fairy set off at once and within an hour she arrived in a chariot of fire pulled by dragons. The King gave her his hand to help her down from the chariot. She said he was right in all he had done. But she had power to see into the future and she thought that when the Princess woke up, she would be very upset to find herself all alone in the old castle. So this is what she did.

With her magic wand she touched everyone in the castle except the King and Queen—governesses, maids of honor, ladies in waiting, gentlemen, officers, stewards, cooks, scullions, errand boys, watchmen, guards, pages, footmen. She also touched all the horses in the stables with their grooms, the big watchdogs in the courtyard, and the Princess's little dog, Puff, who was next to her on the bed. As soon as she touched them they all fell asleep. They would only wake up at the same moment as their mistress. Then they would be all ready to wait on her when she needed them. Even the roasting spits on the fire that were full of partridges and pheasants went to sleep. So did the fire. It was all done in a moment. Fairies do not take long to do their work.

Then the King and Queen kissed their darling child, without waking her up, and left the castle. They made laws forbidding anyone to come near it. But these laws were not needed. Within a quarter of an hour, so many trees, both large and small, sprang up all around the park with brambles and thorns twined together that neither man nor beast could get through. Only the tops of the castle towers could be seen from far off. This was another of the fairy's magic spells so that the Princess would have nothing to fear from prying people while she was asleep.

At the end of a hundred years, when a different family from that of the sleeping Princess was on the throne, the King's son went hunting that way. Seeing the towers rising above the thickly tangled wood, he asked what they were. Each person told him what he had heard—some said it was an old castle haunted by ghosts, others that all the witches in the neighborhood held their revels there. The most common opinion was that an ogre lived there and brought there all the children he could catch in order to eat them at his leisure. No one could follow him there because he alone had the power to make a pathway through the woods.

The Prince did not know what to believe until an old peasant spoke up and said:

"Prince, more than fifty years ago I heard my father say that in that castle lies a princess, the most beautiful ever to be seen. She must sleep for a hundred years

and then she will be wakened by a King's son whom she has been waiting for."

When the young Prince heard this he felt as if he were on fire. He was sure that he was the one to bring this fine adventure to its end. Love and glory inspired him there and then to see for himself what was really there. He had hardly begun to go toward the woods when all the huge trees, the brambles and the thorns bent aside by themselves to let him pass. He walked on toward the castle that he could see at the end of a great avenue of trees. Then to his surprise he saw that none of his men had been able to follow him, because as soon as he had passed by the trees entwined themselves together again. But a young prince in love is always brave, so he did not hesitate to go on.

He entered a large forecourt, and at once the things he saw were enough to make hm icy with fear. There was a dreadful silence. Death seemed to be all around him with the bodies of men and animals lying as if they were dead. Yet he could tell by the pimply noses and red faces of the watchmen that they were only asleep. Their glasses still held a few drops of wine that showed they had fallen asleep as they were drinking.

He passed through a great courtyard paved with marble. He climbed the stairs. He went into the room where the guards were lined up, guns on their shoulders, snoring as hard as they could. He crossed many more rooms full of gentlemen and ladies in waiting, some standing, some sitting but all of them asleep. Then at last he came to a room all decorated with gold. The curtains round the bed were drawn aside, and there he saw the most beautiful sight he had ever seen—a Princess, who seemed to be about fifteen or sixteen years old, whose shimmering beauty seemed almost unearthly. Trembling with wonder, he drew near and knelt down beside her.

At this moment the spell was brought to an end. The Princess woke up. She looked at him with eyes more full of tenderness than you would have expected for a first glance:

"Is it you, my Prince?" she said. "You have been so long in coming."

Charmed by these words and, even more, by the way in which they were spoken, the Prince scarcely knew how to show her his joy and gratitude. He swore he loved her better than he loved himself. His speech was faltering but pleased her none the less for that. The less fluent our words the stronger are our feelings. He was more embarrassed than she was, but that is hardly surprising. She had had time to dream about what she was going to say to him. (Though the story says nothing about it, it looks as if the good fairy brought her beautiful dreams during her long sleep.) And so they talked together for hours on end, and still they had not said half the things they wanted to say.

Meanwhile the whole palace had awakened with the Princess. Each person went about his work but, since they were not in love, they began to die of hunger.

68

The chief lady in waiting, who felt just as starving as the others, lost her patience and said to the Princess in a loud voice that supper was served. As the Prince helped the Princess to get up, he saw that she was already fully clothed with great magnificence. But he was careful not to tell her that she was dressed in the old-fashioned style of his grandmother with a high collar. She looked none the less beautiful for that.

They went into a room all hung with mirrors and had their supper, served by the Princess's stewards. Violins and oboes played old tunes that had not been heard for nearly a hundred years but were still very fine. After supper, without wasting any time, the chaplain married them in the castle chapel and the chief lady in waiting drew the curtains round their bed. They slept little. The Princess did not need much sleep and the Prince had to leave her as soon as it was morning to go back to the town. His father would be anxious about him.

The Prince told him that while he was out hunting he had lost his way in the forest and slept the night in a charcoal burner's hut, eating black bread and cheese for his supper. The King, who was a kind man, believed him. But his mother was not so easy to convince. When she saw that he went out hunting nearly every day and always had a good excuse for spending two or three nights away, she felt sure that he was busy with some love affair. He lived with the Princess like this for more than two whole years and they had two children. The first was a daughter called Dawn, the second a son called Day because he was even better looking than his sister.

Many times the Queen tried to make her son confide in her by saying that it was right for people to enjoy life. But he never dared tell her his secret. Although he loved her he was afraid of her because she came from a family of ogres. The King had only married her for her riches. It was even whispered at court that she still had ogrish longings and that when she saw little children go by she could hardly keep from pouncing on them. So the Prince did not want to tell her anything.

But after two years the King died and the Prince became master. He announced his marriage publicly and went with great ceremony to fetch his wife, the Queen, from her castle. The capital city gave her a royal welcome when she arrived with her two children on either side.

Some time later the King went to war with his neighbor, the Emperor Cantalabutt. He left the kingdom in charge of his mother the Queen, asking her to take great care of his wife and children. He had to be at war for the whole summer. As soon as he had gone the Queen Mother sent her daughter-in-law and her children to a country house in the woods. There she thought she would be able to satisfy her horrible craving more easily. A few days later she went there herself and said to her steward:

"Tomorrow I want to eat little Dawn for my dinner."

"But, madam . . ." said the steward.

"That is my wish," said the Queen in the voice of an ogress who wants to eat human flesh, "and I want to eat her with mustard sauce."

The poor man realized that it was no good trifling with an ogress. He took up his carving knife and went up to little Dawn's room. She was then four years old and she came up to him laughing and skipping. She threw her arms round his neck and asked him for a sweet. He began to cry and the knife fell from his hand. He went down again to the farmyard and killed a lamb, which he served up with such a delicious sauce that his mistress said she had never eaten anything so good. At the same time he took little Dawn down to his wife so that she could hide her away in her rooms at the back of the yard.

Eight days later the wicked Queen said to the steward:

"I want to eat little Day for my supper."

He did not answer because he planned to trick her as he had done before. He went to look for little Day and found him with a toy sword in his hand, playing at fighting with a pet monkey. He was only three years old. He carried him down to his wife who hid him away with little Dawn. Then the steward cooked a tender young kid in his place, which the ogress found delicious.

All had gone well so far, but one evening the wicked Queen said to the steward:

"I want to eat the Queen served with the same sauce as her children."

Then the poor steward began to despair of tricking her yet again. The young Queen was more than twenty years old, not counting the hundred years she had been asleep, and though her skin was still lovely and white it was a bit tough. How could he find a farmyard animal as tough as that? In order to save his own life, he made up his mind to cut the young Queen's throat and he went up to her room with the intention of getting the job done quickly. Working himself into a rage, he rushed into the young Queen's room, dagger in hand. But he did not want to give her a fright so, with great respect, he told her about the order he had received from the Queen Mother.

"Do it, do it," she cried, baring her throat to him. "Carry out the order you have been given. I will go to join my children, the poor children I loved so much!"

She thought they were dead because they had been taken away without a word said to her.

"No, no, madam," said the poor steward, overcome with pity. "You shall not die and you will see your children again. You will see them at my house where I have hidden them away. I will trick the Queen yet again by giving her a young deer to eat in your place."

Then he took her at once to his rooms. Leaving her there to hug her children and cry over them, he went to prepare the deer. The Queen ate it for supper with as much relish as if it had been the young Queen herself. She was very pleased with her cruelty and she planned to tell the King on his return that savage wolves had eaten his wife and children.

One evening, when she was prowling about as usual round the courtyards of the castle to see if she could smell some fresh human flesh, she heard little Day crying in a room downstairs. His mother wanted to spank him because he had been naughty. Then she heard little Dawn begging forgiveness for her brother. The ogress recognized the voices of the Queen and her children and she was furious because she had been tricked. The next morning, in a dreadful voice that made everyone tremble, she commanded a huge vat to be brought into the courtyard and filled with toads, vipers, adders and other poisonous snakes. She ordered the Queen and her children, the steward and his wife and servant all to be led out with their hands tied behind their backs so that they could be thrown into it.

There they all stood with the executioners ready to throw them into the vat, when the King, who was not expected back so soon, rode into the courtyard. He had traveled fast and, in amazement, demanded to know what this horrible sight meant. Nobody dared to tell him, when suddenly the ogress, enraged at what was happening, threw herself headfirst into the vat. In an instant she was devoured by the horrible creatures she had had put in there. The King could not help being upset, after all she was his mother. But he soon consoled himself with his beautiful wife and his children.

MORAL

Waiting awhile to find a husband
Rich and handsome, gentle and kind,
This, you will say, is natural enough.
But where will you find a girl so patient
That she would wait for him asleep
A hundred years until he comes?

This story seems to mean, you see,
That marriage ties are no less sweet
However long we wait for them:
Nothing is lost by being patient.

But girls are filled with so much longing
To have a husband as soon as they can,
That I haven't the heart to preach a moral
I know they do not want to hear.

TALES OF MOTHER GOOSE

Patient Griselda

At the foot of the mountains in the valley of the river Po, there lived a young and valiant Prince who had all the gifts of mind and body that Heaven could give. He was strong in war but enjoyed the arts as well. He loved battles and brave deeds but, above all, he loved his people. There was only one shadow on his character. Deep in his heart he believed that women were faithless and deceitful. However charming they might be on the surface, he was sure that, once married, they turned into dreadful tyrants.

The Prince swore he would never marry. Each day, after he had spent the morning looking after the welfare of his subjects, helping poor widows and protecting orphans, he went off hunting. He was much less frightened of savage bears and wild boars than he was of women's wiles. However, his subjects urged him constantly to marry, in order to give them an heir who would rule the kingdom as benevolently as he did.

One day, they sent a deputation to him in a last effort to persuade him to change his mind, urging him with all their might to give them a successor. In a quiet voice the Prince replied:

"I am touched that you should concern yourselves so deeply over my marriage. I wish I could oblige you by marrying tomorrow. But just look what happens! Charming young girls, who were the sweetest creatures imaginable at home with their parents, are no sooner married and sure of their man, than they change out of all recognition. Some become flirts and never have enough lovers to satisfy them, others are bluestockings, and some become such wild gamblers that they end up losing all their jewelry, their furniture, even the clothes they are wearing. Above all, they want to rule the roost. So if you want me to marry, you must find some young beauty without pride or vanity, very patient and obedient, with no will of her own. If you can find such a person, I will marry her."

So saying, the Prince leaped onto his horse and galloped off to join the hunt. The hounds ran barking through the woods, the horses neighed and the huntsmen blew their horns so loudly that the forest echoed to the sound. By chance, the Prince took a side path that led away from all the noise of hunting into a pleasant meadow with a stream running through it. And suddenly there appeared before his eyes the loveliest sight he had ever seen in his life. It was a young shepherdess watching over her sheep by the side of the stream. She would have tamed the most savage heart with her beautiful blue eyes. The noise of the Prince's horse startled her and, when she saw there was someone looking at her, she blushed deeply. Her innocence and simplicity charmed the Prince, who felt just as shy as she did. He asked her if she had seen his huntsmen pass that way. She said she had not, but she would put him on the right path back to the forest. He bent down to quench his thirst from the stream, and quickly she fetched him a cup and filled it for him to drink. On the way home he made a map in his mind's eye of all the paths he went along so as to be sure to find his way again.

The next day he felt so sad at being far away from the beautiful girl that, as soon as he could, he went hunting again. Slipping away from the hunt he once more found his way to the young shepherdess's hut. He learned that she lived alone with her father and that Griselda was her name. And the more he saw of her, the more sure he was that her character was as sweet and gentle as her face. Back at the palace he called his council to him and said:

"According to your wishes, I have decided to marry. I will not choose a wife from a foreign country, I will choose one from among our own people. But I will not tell you who it is until the wedding day."

Great was the excitement as the news spread all round the kingdom, and the people were overjoyed. All the young beauties of the town hoped that his choice might fall on them. Having heard that he was looking for a chaste and modest wife, they changed their clothes to seem more like his ideal. They softened their voices, let their fair fall loosely round them, put on high-necked dresses with long sleeves, so that only their little fingers showed.

Great preparations were made to decorate the city for the wedding celebrations. At last the great day arrived. People began to gather on all sides and the palace rang to the sound of flutes, drums and trumpets. At last the Prince came out surrounded by his courtiers, and a loud cheer went up. But, much to everyone's surprise, he took the same path he usually took to go hunting. His courtiers followed him in amazement as he cantered through the forest and down the winding paths until at length he came to Griselda's hut.

Griselda had heard of the wedding celebrations and was just getting ready to set out to go and see the ceremony.

"Where are you off to?" asked the Prince, looking tenderly at her. "Don't hurry away, sweet shepherdess. The wedding you are going to is my own and it will not take place without you. I love you and I have chosen you, out of all the beauties in my kingdom, to spend the rest of my life with, if you will have me."

"Oh sir," she said, "such glory is not for me. You're making fun of me."

"No, no," said he, "I'm quite sincere. I have already spoken to your father. But first, to make quite sure that we will live in peace together, swear to me that you will never go against my wishes."

"I swear it," she said. "Even if I had married a humble village boy, I would gladly have obeyed him. So how could I fail to obey you, since you will be both my king and my husband?"

Then the courtiers dressed her in the fine clothes and jewels they had brought with them, and she took her place beside the Prince in a gold and ivory chariot. Back they went to the town and the marriage took place.

Griselda seemed to know by instinct how to behave as a queen. Everything she did was right. And after a year she gave birth to a lovely daughter. But the Prince fell into a black mood and his old suspicions of women came back to him. He suspected all her behavior and thought she was trying to deceive him. In order to test her out, he had her shut up in her room and rudely took away all the pearls and rubies and other jewels he had given her. Griselda said to herself that he was trying her out to test her constancy, but when he saw how meekly she obeyed him he decided to go even further. He ordered that her child should be taken away from her and brought up apart. Secretly he had her sent to a convent to be looked after by the nuns. Then Griselda was told she had died. Great was her sorrow but, in spite of her own grief, her only thought was to comfort her husband. The Prince was so moved by her devotion that he was on the point of telling her the truth, but his pride prevented him.

Fifteen years passed and the young Princess grew into a great beauty. By chance a young nobleman saw her at a window and fell violently in love with her, and the Princess returned his love. The Prince was pleased with the match but he determined to test out the young lovers and, at the same time, to put a final test to the patience of his wife.

"A little uncertainty will make their love all the stronger. As for my wife, I can no longer doubt her love. But this test will prove her great virtues to all the world, and her fame will spread far and wide."

He announced publicly that, since his only daughter had died at birth, he must marry again to provide an heir to the throne. He said he had chosen the young

girl who had been brought up in the convent. You can imagine what effect the cruel news had on the young lovers. Then he told his faithful wife that his people wished him to marry again.

"You must go back to your hut," he said, "wearing your old shepherdess's clothes."

"You are my husband, my lord and master," she said, almost fainting. "However terrible the things you tell me to do, you know my only pleasure is to obey you." She went up to her room and, taking off her rich gown, put on her rough clothes again. Then she said to the Prince:

"Before I leave, please forgive me for having displeased you. With your forgiveness I will live content in my sad exile. My love for you will never change."

At this the Prince nearly changed his mind but he resolved to go on with his plan and sent her away. Shortly afterward he sent for her again to ask her to get the rooms ready for his new bride, whom he showed to the Princess. As soon as she saw the beautiful girl, Griselda was filled with maternal love. She remembered the child she had lost and reflected that, had she lived she would be just the same age and, perhaps, as beautiful as this girl. Griselda begged the Prince to treat her gently, for she had been delicately brought up and would not be able to stand the rough treatment she had had from him. A harsh word might break her heart. The Prince only told her severely to mind her own business.

When the wedding guests had all arrived the Prince assembled them all together and said:

"Do not be deceived by appearances. You might think that this lovely young girl, who is about to become my Princess, would have a happy heart. She has not. You might think that this young nobleman, so full of brave deeds and valor, would enjoy seeing the wedding. It is not true. You would think that Griselda has every reason to weep with anger. But she does not. She has given her consent to everything and never lost patience. Now I must tell you that, were I to be married as I had planned, I would be the most miserable of princes. For this young girl is my daughter. Instead, I give her hand to this young nobleman who loves her and who she loves in return. As for myself, for the rest of my life I will love and cherish the faithful wife that I sent away so cruelly. My only thought will be to make her happy and I want the memory of her virtue never to be forgotten."

Then the three people who had been so unhappy before broke into smiles of joy. The young Princess threw herself at her father's feet. He lifted her up, kissed her and led her to her mother. Griselda had borne all her worst misfortunes with fortitude, but this great happiness was too much for her. She put her arms round her daughter and could not stop weeping.

Then the marriage was celebrated. There was dancing and music and feasting, and all eyes were on Griselda whose praises were sung above all others. The people were so pleased with their Prince that they even thought his cruelty was no bad thing since it had given rise to such a model of patience.

The Ridiculous Wishes

ONCE UPON A TIME there was a poor woodcutter who was so weary of his hard life that he only wanted to die. In his grief he complained that Heaven had never granted a single one of his wishes. One day, when he was in the woods sorrowing about his lot, Jupiter appeared to him with his thunderbolt in his hand. The poor man was terrified. "I don't want anything," he cried, throwing himself to the ground. "I'll drop my wishes if you'll drop your thunderbolt. Live and let live."

"Don't be afraid," said Jupiter. "I heard your complaints and I've come to show you how wrong you are about me. Listen. I, master of all the world, promise to grant you the first three wishes you make, whatever they are. Think hard about what you really want because all your happiness depends on it."

With these words Jupiter went back to heaven, and the woodcutter gaily threw his bundle of wood over his shoulder and went home.

"I mustn't decide anything carelessly," he said to himself as he trotted along. "It's so important that I must ask my wife's advice. Fanny," he called out as he reached his thatched cottage, "make up the fire and prepare a good meal. We are rich for life. We only have to make three wishes."

Then he told his wife all that had happened. At once she began to think of all kinds of extravagant ideas. Then, remembering how important it was to choose carefully, she said to her husband:

"Blaise, my dear, don't let's get impatient. We must think things over carefully. Let's sleep on it and leave our first wish till tomorrow."

"Just what I think," said Blaise. "Now go and fetch me the wine behind the woodpile." When she came back he had a good drink and, leaning back in his chair, stretched his legs in front of the fire saying, "I wish I had a nice big sausage

to cook over this fine blaze." No sooner had he said these words than, to her astonishment, his wife saw a long sausage coming out from a corner of the chimney and snaking toward her. She gave a cry then, realizing that it was all because of the wish her stupid husband had made, she began to shout at him:

"You could have had an empire, with gold and pearls and rubies and diamonds and beautiful clothes, and all you wished for was a sausage!"

"Yes, I was wrong," he said, "I was wrong. I wished for the wrong thing. I'll do better next time."

"So you say," she went on. "Only a stupid oaf could have made a wish like that."

Her husband flew into a rage, almost wishing under his breath that she was dead (and perhaps he would have been better off if she had been). Out loud he said:

"What a life! To hell with this sausage, I wish it would stick to your nose."

His wish was heard immediately. No sooner had the words left his mouth, than the sausage stuck to the end of his angry wife's nose. It annoyed her very much. Fanny was rather pretty and charming to look at and, to tell the truth, she was not improved by this ornament dangling from her nose. The only advantage was that, as it hung down over her mouth, it stopped her talking. Her husband began to think that he hadn't made such a bad wish after all.

"After all these mistakes," he said to himself, "perhaps I'd better use my last wish to turn myself into a king. It's true that nothing could be finer than to be a king, but what about my queen? How miserable she would be, sitting on the throne with a nose a yard long. I'd better ask her what she thinks, whether she'd rather be a grand princess with a horrible great nose, or whether she'd rather remain a wood-cutter's wife with a nose like she had before."

Fanny thought about it hard. She knew that queens are always flattered and told their noses are perfect, whatever they look like. But, in spite of this, her desire to look pretty was stronger than anything else. She preferred to be as she was, rather than turn into an ugly queen.

So the woodcutter remained a woodcutter. He didn't become a grand potentate. His purse was not filled with gold. He was only too glad to use his last wish to turn his wife back into her old self.

So you see, men, however miserable and disgruntled they are, are not very good at making wishes. And very few of them know how to make proper use of the talents God has given them.

Donkey Skin

Once upon a time there was a great King who was so loved by his people and so respected by his neighbors and allies that he was the happiest of monarchs. His happiness was made even greater by choosing for his queen a most beautiful and virtuous princess. Their marriage was perfect, and their daughter was so lovely and so full of charm that they did not mind having no more children.

Their palace was spacious and magnificent. Their ministers were clever and wise, their courtiers virtuous, their servants faithful and hard-working. In their huge stables were the finest horses in the world with richly embroidered saddles. But strangers who came to admire these marvelous stables were amazed. For in the center stood a donkey, waving his enormous ears. It was no whim on the part of the King to put him in the place of honor. He did it with good reason. For the virtues of this rare creature certainly deserved the honor. Nature had made him in such a way that, instead of dropping manure onto the straw, he covered it with gold coins which were collected each morning.

Unfortunately, life is just as uncertain for kings as for their subjects, bad things are mixed with good. It so happened that the Queen was quite suddenly taken seriously ill. No doctors could cure her and everyone was grief-stricken. The King, who loved her dearly (in spite of the famous proverb that says that marriage is the grave of love), was overcome with sorrow. He offered prayers in all the holy shrines of his kingdom and wanted to give his own life in place of his wife's. But he begged the gods and the fairies in vain. As the Queen felt her last hour approaching, she said to her weeping husband:

"Before I die, I want you to promise one thing. If you want to marry again . . ."

At these words the King sobbed pitifully, seizing his wife's hands and covering them with tears, assuring her that it was out of the question to talk of a second marriage:

"No, no, my darling Queen," he said, "it's more likely that I shall follow you into the grave."

"The state needs successors," said the Queen firmly. "As I have only given you one daughter, you need to have sons like you. But I want you to swear, by all the love you have for me, not to give in to the people's demands for you to marry until you have found a princess more beautiful than I am. Give me your word and then I will die happy."

I presume that the Queen made him promise this because she did not think there was anyone to equal her in all the world. (She was a little conceited.) She thought that he would not be able to marry again. Then she died, and no husband ever made such a racket as the King. He wept and sobbed day and night, thinking of nothing but his widowhood.

Great sorrows do not last. By and by his nobles had a meeting and came in a body to beg the King to marry again. This suggestion seemed heartless to the King and started him crying all over again. He reminded them of the promise he had made to his Queen and defied them to find a princess more beautiful than his wife, thinking it quite impossible. But the councilors dismissed such a promise as rubbish. What did beauty matter, they said, as long as the queen was virtuous and able to have children? They said that the state needed princes to ensure the succession. They said that although his daughter had all the right qualifications to make a great queen, she would have to choose a foreigner for a husband. Then, either he would take her away to live in his country or, if he reigned with her, their children would not be of the right blood. And, since there would be no prince bearing the King's name, the neighboring peoples would start warring and ruin the kingdom. The King was taken aback by all their arguments and promised to think what he could do to satisfy them.

So he searched among all the marriageable princesses to find one that would suit him. Every day they brought him charming portraits to look at, but not one had the qualities of his Queen. He could not make up his mind. Unfortunately he began to think that his daughter, the Princess, was not only ravishingly beautiful but even more talented and delightful than her mother. Her youth and the freshness of her lovely complexion set the King on fire. He could not hide his feelings from the young Princess and told her that he had decided to marry her because she was the only one who fulfilled the conditions of his promise to the Queen.

The young Princess, who was very virtuous and shy, thought she would faint at this horrible suggestion. She threw herself at her father's feet, begging him with all her might not to force her to commit such a horrible crime.

But once the King had got this extraordinary idea into his head, he called on an old druid to soothe the Princess's conscience. This druid was more ambitious than religious and he was quite prepared to sacrifice the Princess's innocence and virtue for the sake of being the confidant of such a great King. He got such a cunning hold over the King's mind, sweetening the crime that he was going to commit, that he even persuaded him that it would be an act of piety to marry his own daughter. The King was flattered by the scoundrel's words and came back more determined than ever with his plan. He ordered the Princess to get ready to do his bidding.

The young Princess, overcome with grief, could think of nothing else to do but to go and see her godmother, the Lilac Fairy. So off she went in the middle of the night in a little carriage drawn by a huge ram who knew all the pathways. She arrived safely and the Lilac Fairy, who loved her, said she knew exactly what she had come to say. She told her not to worry because no harm could come to her if she did exactly as she told her:

"My dearest child," she said, "it would be very wrong to marry your father. But without having to refuse him openly, you can put him off. Tell him that, to please you, he must give you a dress that is the color of the sky. With all his love and all his power he will never be able to do it."

The Princess thanked her godmother. And the next day she spoke to the King just as the fairy had advised her, saying that she could not agree to marry him unless she could have a dress the color of the sky.

The King was delighted to have even the hope of her acceptance, and commanded his most skillful tailors to make her the dress, otherwise they would all be hung. No sky could be a more beautiful blue than this lovely dress when it was spread out before her. The Princess was very upset and did not know how to get out of her embarrassment. The King pressed her to agree to the wedding. Once again she had to run to her godmother, who was amazed that her secret advice had not succeeded. This time she told her to ask for a dress the color of the moon. The King could refuse her nothing. He sent for his finest workmen and ordered them to make a dress the color of the moon.

The Princess was delighted with the dress but not with her father's attentions. She wept even more as soon as she was alone with her nurse and her ladies in waiting. Then the fairy, who knew everything, came to her help and said:

"If you ask for a dress the color of the sun, I don't think even your father could manage to have one made. And, at least, we will gain a little more time."

The Princess asked her father for the dress, and he was so much in love that he gave all the diamonds and rubies out of his crown to be embroidered onto the dress with the order that nothing should be spared to make it as brilliant as the sun. As soon as it was ready, everyone who saw it had to shut their eyes because they

88

were so dazzled. This is when dark glasses first had to be used. What did the Princess think of it? No one had ever seen such exquisite workmanship. She was dumfounded. With the excuse that her eyes were hurting, she went back to her room where the fairy was waiting, rather ashamed of herself. When she had seen the dress as dazzling as the sun she grew red with anger:

"Very well, my girl," she said to the Princess, "we'll put your father's love to a terrible test. I know how obstinate he is about this marriage, but I think even he will be stunned by what I advise you to ask him next. Ask him for the skin of that donkey he's so fond of, the one that gives him such riches—off you go, and don't forget to ask him that."

The Princess was delighted to have found a way of escaping the marriage she detested. She did not imagine for a moment that her father would sacrifice his donkey, so she told him that she longed for the skin of this magnificent animal. Although the King was astonished at her wish, he did not hesitate to grant it. The poor donkey was killed and his skin carried to the Princess. She could see no way out of her misfortune and was getting desperate when her godmother came running:

"What are you doing, my girl?" she said, seeing the Princess tearing her hair and scratching her cheeks. "This is the finest moment of your life. Wrap yourself in this skin, leave the palace and go as far away as you can. When we sacrifice all we have to virtue, then the gods will reward us. Go quickly and I will make sure that your clothes and your jewels follow after you. Wherever you go, this chest will follow you under the ground. Here is my magic wand. Whenever you need the chest, just tap the ground and it will appear. But make haste to go now, don't delay."

The Princess kissed her godmother a hundred times and begged her not to abandon her. Then she wrapped herself in the ugly skin, blacking her face with soot from the chimney, and left the palace without being recognized by anyone.

The Princesses's absence caused a huge row. The King, in despair, could not be consoled. He had prepared a magnificent wedding celebration. Now he sent a hundred guards and more than a thousand soldiers to look for his daughter. But the fairy protected her and made her invisible to the cunningest searchers.

Meanwhile the Princess walked on and on. No matter how far she went, she could not find a place to stay. Because, although people gave her something to eat out of charity, she was so filthy that they would not take her in. One day she came to a fine town, on the edge of which there was a farm. The farmer's wife needed a scullery maid to wash the clothes and clean out the turkeys and the pigsty. When this woman saw how scruffy she was, she invited her to come in. The Princess accepted gladly because she was so worn out with traveling. They put her in a dark corner of the kitchen and, for the first few days, she was the butt of all the servants' jokes because the donkey skin made her so dirty and repulsive. At length they got used to it. And she was so good at doing all her jobs that the farmer's wife took her under her wing. She took the sheep out to graze and brought them back at the right time. She looked after the turkeys as if she'd never done anything else. And they all flourished in her care.

One day when she was sitting beside a clear spring, where she often came to think of her unhappy state, she looked at herself in the water and the horrible donkey skin that she was dressed in shocked her. Ashamed of her appearance, she washed her face and hands and they became as white as ivory, while her face showed all its natural beauty. Her joy at finding herself pretty again made her want to bathe all over, which she did. But she had to put her dirty skin on again to go back to the farm.

Luckily, the next day was a holiday. So she had time to get out her chest and arrange all her things, to brush her beautiful hair and put on her sky-blue dress. Her room was so small that there was hardly room for the train of the long dress. The beautiful Princess looked at herself in the mirror and was so pleased with what she saw that she decided to amuse herself by putting on all her lovely dresses in turn on Sundays and holidays. And so she did. She carefully twined flowers and diamonds in her hair. And often she wished that there was someone to see her beauty, not just the sheep and turkeys that liked her just as well in her horrible donkey skin. They named her after it on the farm.

One holiday when Donkey Skin had put on her golden dress, the King's son, who owned the farm, came back that way from hunting and got down from his horse to rest. The Prince was young and very handsome, beloved by his father and the Queen his mother and adored by all his people. They gave the Prince some refreshment out of doors, and then he began to explore the courtyard and all the nooks and corners. Going from place to place, he went down a dark passage at the bottom of which he saw a closed door. Curiosity made him put his eye to the keyhole. To his amazement he saw a princess so beautiful and so magnificently dressed, with so noble and modest an air, that he took her for a goddess. The strength of his feelings at that moment nearly made him push open the door. But the respect he felt for the delightful person inside held him back.

Hard as it was for him to drag himself away from the dark passage, he did so in order to find out who it was who lived in the little room. They told him it was a scullery maid called Donkey Skin because of the skin she wore. She was so ugly and foul that no one took any notice of her or spoke to her. They had taken her in out of pity to look after the sheep and the turkeys.

The Prince was not satisfied with this explanation. But he saw that these rough people did not know any better and it was no use questioning them. He went back to his father's palace madly in love, with the vision constantly before his eyes of the

miraculous person he had seen through the keyhole. He wished he had knocked on the door and promised himself that he would the next time. But the strength of his passion made him fall into a fever that same night, which soon made him dangerously ill. He was his mother's only child and she despaired of his being cured. In vain she promised great rewards to the doctors. They did their best, but nothing could cure the Prince.

At length they discovered that it was a mortal grief that was causing his illness. They told the Queen. Full of tenderness for her son, she begged him to tell her the cause of his grief. If it was because he wanted the crown, then the King his father would gladly step down from the throne and put him in his place. If he was in love with some princess, then they would give him his heart's desire, even if they were at war with her father. They would sacrifice anything to please him. But she begged him not to die because her very life depended on his. All this the Queen told the Prince, sprinkling his face with her tears.

"Madam," said the Prince at last in a weak voice, "I am not so unnatural as to want my father's crown. God grant that he should live for many more years and that he should know me to be the most loyal and respectful of all his subjects! As for princesses, I have not yet thought of marrying, and you know that I would always obey your wishes on the matter, whatever it might cost me."

"Oh, my son," replied the Queen. "I would do anything to save your life. I beg you to save mine and your father the King's, by telling us what it is you want. Rest assured that we will grant it to you."

"Well, madam," he said, "since I must tell you my longing, I will obey you. It would be a crime to endanger the lives of the two people most dear to me. Mother, I want Donkey Skin to make me a cake. And when it is made, I want her to bring it to me."

The Queen was astonished at this extraordinary name and asked who this Donkey Skin was.

"Madam," replied one of her officers who happened to have seen the girl. "She's the ugliest creature imaginable after the wolf. She's a filthy, ragged girl who lodges at the farm and looks after the turkeys."

"Never mind," said the Queen, "perhaps my son ate one of her cakes on his way back from hunting. It's just a sick man's whim. Since there is such a person as Donkey Skin, I want this Donkey Skin to make him a cake at once."

Off he ran to the farm to find Donkey Skin and ordered her to do her best to make a cake for the Prince.

Some people say that when the Prince put his eye to the keyhole, Donkey Skin saw it. She looked out of her window later and saw such a young and handsome prince that she could not forget him and sighed for him many times afterward. However that may be, Donkey Skin had either seen him or heard people talk of him with such praise that she was delighted to find a way of making herself known. She shut herself in her room, took off the ugly skin, washed her face and hands, brushed her fair hair, put on her silver blouse with a matching skirt and began to make the cake he longed for. She used pure white flour, eggs and fresh butter. As she worked, somehow or other (it might have been on purpose) a ring fell off her finger into the bowl and got mixed into the cake. As soon as it was cooked she put on her horrible skin. She gave the cake to the officer and she asked him for news of the Prince. He did not deign to reply, but ran straight to the Prince to bring him the cake.

The Prince took it greedily from the officer's hands and began to eat it so ravenously that the doctors who were there told each other that this was a very bad sign. Indeed, the Prince thought he was going to choke on the ring he found in one of the pieces of cake. But he carefully took it out of his mouth and, as he examined it, his eagerness to devour the cake left him. The ring was a fine emerald set in gold, and it was so small that he thought it would only fit the prettiest finger in the world.

He kissed the ring a thousand times and hid it under his pillow, bringing it out again whenever he thought no one was looking. He was tormented by wondering how he could get to see the person the ring belonged to. He did not think for a moment that he could ask for Donkey Skin, who had made the cake, to be brought to him. Nor did he dare tell them what he had seen through the keyhole, because he thought they would tease him and say he was seeing visions. All these thoughts tortured him at once so that the fever took hold of him again. The doctors, not knowing what more to do, told the Queen that the Prince was dying of love. At once she and the King rushed to their son.

"My dear son," cried the King, very upset, "tell us the name of the person you love. We swear to you that you shall have her, even if she is the filthiest slut in the world."

The Queen kissed her son and confirmed what the King had said. Then the Prince, who was touched by his parents' tears, said:

"Dear father and mother, I don't want to make a marriage that would displease you. To prove it, I promise to marry the person whose finger fits this ring." So saying he took the ring from under his pillow. "Someone with a finger as finely made as that could not possibly be a loutish peasant girl."

The King and Queen took the ring and examined it curiously. They, too, like the Prince, agreed that the ring could only fit a well-born lady. Then the King kissed his son, begging him to get better, and ordered his drummers and trumpeters to march round all the town with the herald proclaiming that whichever girl the ring fitted perfectly should marry the heir to the throne.

Princesses were the first to arrive, then duchesses, marquesses and baronesses. But, however much they squeezed and pinched, not one of them could put on the ring. Next, the dressmakers tried it on but, pretty though they were, their fingers were too fat. The Prince, who felt a bit better, held the ring out himself. Then they called for the chambermaids, and they fared no better. They went on trying till no one was left. They had tried all the cooks, the kitchen maids and the shepherd girls, but the ring got stuck on the nails of their fat, red fingers.

"Has anyone fetched Donkey Skin who made me a cake the other day?" asked the Prince. Everyone began to laugh and they told him no, she was much too dirty and foul.

"Go and fetch her at once," ordered the King. "I shall not have it said that I left anyone out."

So off they went, laughing and joking, to fetch the girl who looked after the turkeys. The Princess, who had heard the drums and the heralds' cries, guessed that it might be her ring that was causing all the racket. She loved the Prince. And, as true love is fearful and hesitant, she was in a continual worry lest some other woman should have a finger as slender as hers. So she was filled with joy when they came knocking at her door to fetch her. As soon as she had heard they were looking for the person whose finger exactly fitted the ring, some wild hope led her to brush her hair as carefully as she could and to put on her beautiful dress with the ruffles of gold lace, studded with emeralds. When she heard them knocking at her door and asking her to come to the palace, she put on her donkey skin and opened the door. The people outside began to mock her, saying that the King was asking for her to be his son's bride. Then, with shouts of laughter, they led her to the Prince. He was astonished at her appearance, unable to believe that this could possibly be the same beautiful girl he had seen dressed with such magnificence. Sad and dismayed at having made a mistake, he said to her:

"Are you the person who lodges at the end of the small passage, beyond the courtyard at the farm?"

"Yes, sir," she replied.

"Show me your hand," he said, trembling and sighing deeply.

What a surprise! The King and Queen and all the chamberlains and court officials were amazed when, from under the filthy black skin, she drew out a delicate little hand, rose-pink and white, whose pretty little finger the ring fitted perfectly.

With a slight movement, the Princess shook off the skin and appeared before them in all her beauty. The Prince, weak as he was, fell at her knees and clasped them with such passion that he made her blush. But it was hardly noticed because the King and Queen rushed to embrace her with all their might and asked her if she would marry their son. The Princess was overcome by the love and caresses of the handsome young Prince and, just as she was going to thank them, the ceiling opened and the Lilac Fairy came down in a chariot made from branches of flowering lilac. With great charm she told the whole story of the Princess.

The King and Queen, delighted to find that Donkey Skin was a great Princess, redoubled their kisses. But the Prince saw more than ever how virtuous she was and his love for her grew with the knowledge. He was so impatient to marry the Princess that he hardly gave them time to make the preparations proper to such a solemn marriage. The King and Queen, who were delighted with their future daughter-in-law, kissed her a thousand times and put their arms around her. But she declared that she could not marry the Prince without her father's permission. At once he was sent the first invitation, without being told who the bride was. The Lilac Fairy presided over all the preparations. Kings came from all countries, some in sedan chairs, some in carriages. The most distant ones came on elephants or on tigers or eagles. But the most magnificent and powerful of all was the Princess's father. Luckily he had forgotten his misguided love for her and he had married a beautiful queen who had been a widow. They had no children. When the Princess ran to meet him, he recognized her at once and kissed her tenderly. The King and Queen presented their son and he treated him with great friendliness. The marriage took place with all the pomp imaginable. But the bride and groom hardly noticed all the show; they had eyes only for each other.

The Prince's father had his son crowned that same day and, kissing his hands, placed him on the throne in spite of his resistance. The Prince had to obey him.

The marriage celebrations lasted for three months. But the Prince and Princess loved each other so much that their love lasted much longer, a hundred years or more if they lived that long.

MORAL

Who knows if Donkey Skin is true,
The tale's so strange and old.
But as long as children like to listen
The story will be told.

THE AUTHOR

CHARLES PERRAULT (1628–1703) enjoyed much fame and success as a wit, author, and scholar in seventeenth-century French literary circles. He is familiar to students of French literature for the prominent role he played in the famous *Quarrel of the Ancients and the Moderns*, which so keenly occupied many men of letters in his day. Today Perrault is best remembered as the author of the traditional fairy tales originally called *Tales of Mother Goose* and *Stories of Olden Times*.

THE TRANSLATOR

SASHA MOORSOM graduated with honors from Cambridge University and she then became a producer for the BBC Third Programme. She is married to the English sociologist, Michael Young, and contributes articles and reviews to various British journals.

THE ILLUSTRATOR

LANDA CROMMELYNCK, a graduate of the prestigious School of Applied Art of Paris, is a young French painter and illustrator. She is married to the famous etcher, Piero Crommelynck, and they live with their daughter in Paris.

DATE DUE

MR 2 4 '90			
JA 02 '90			
AP 13 '91			